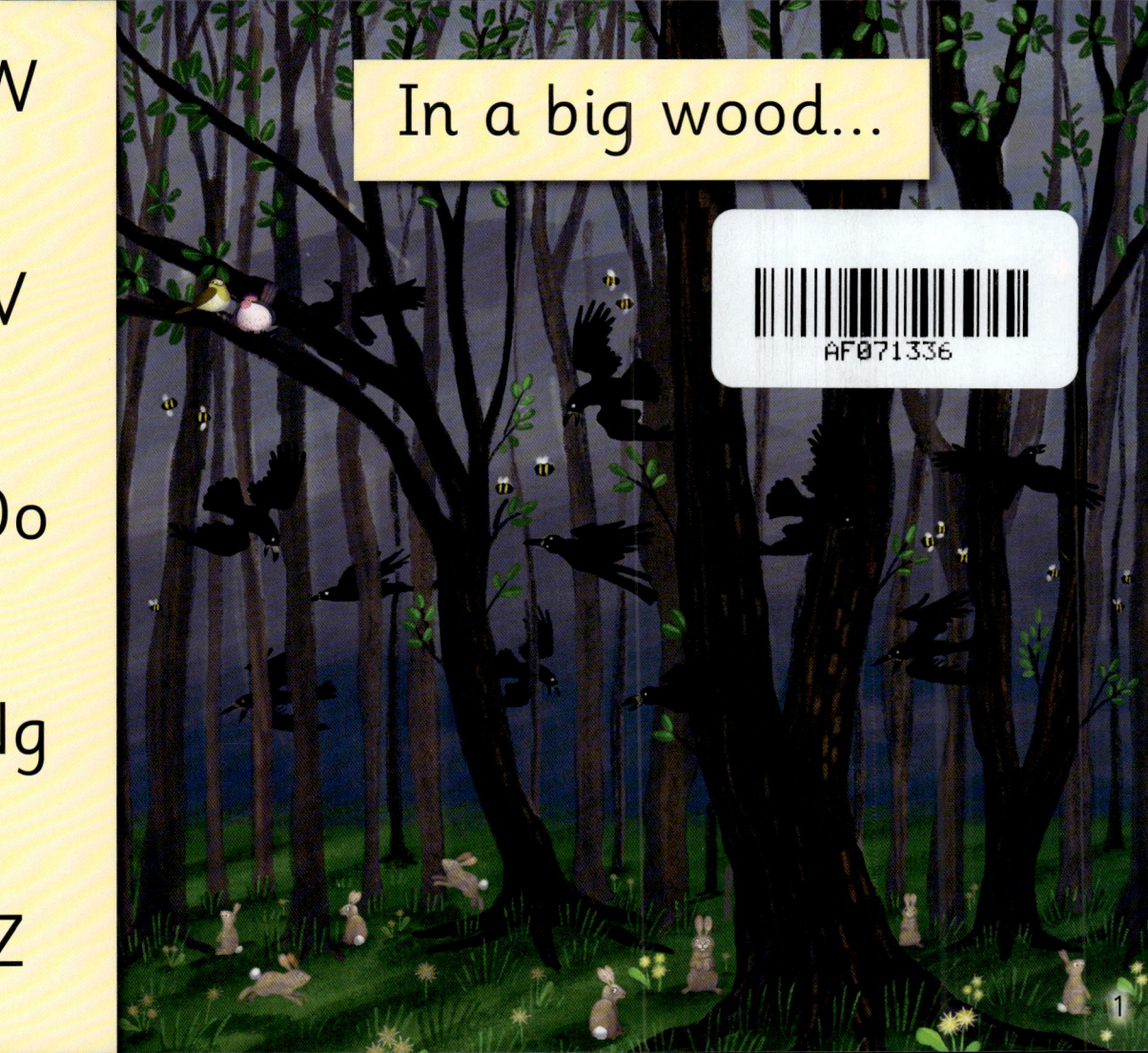

In a big wood...

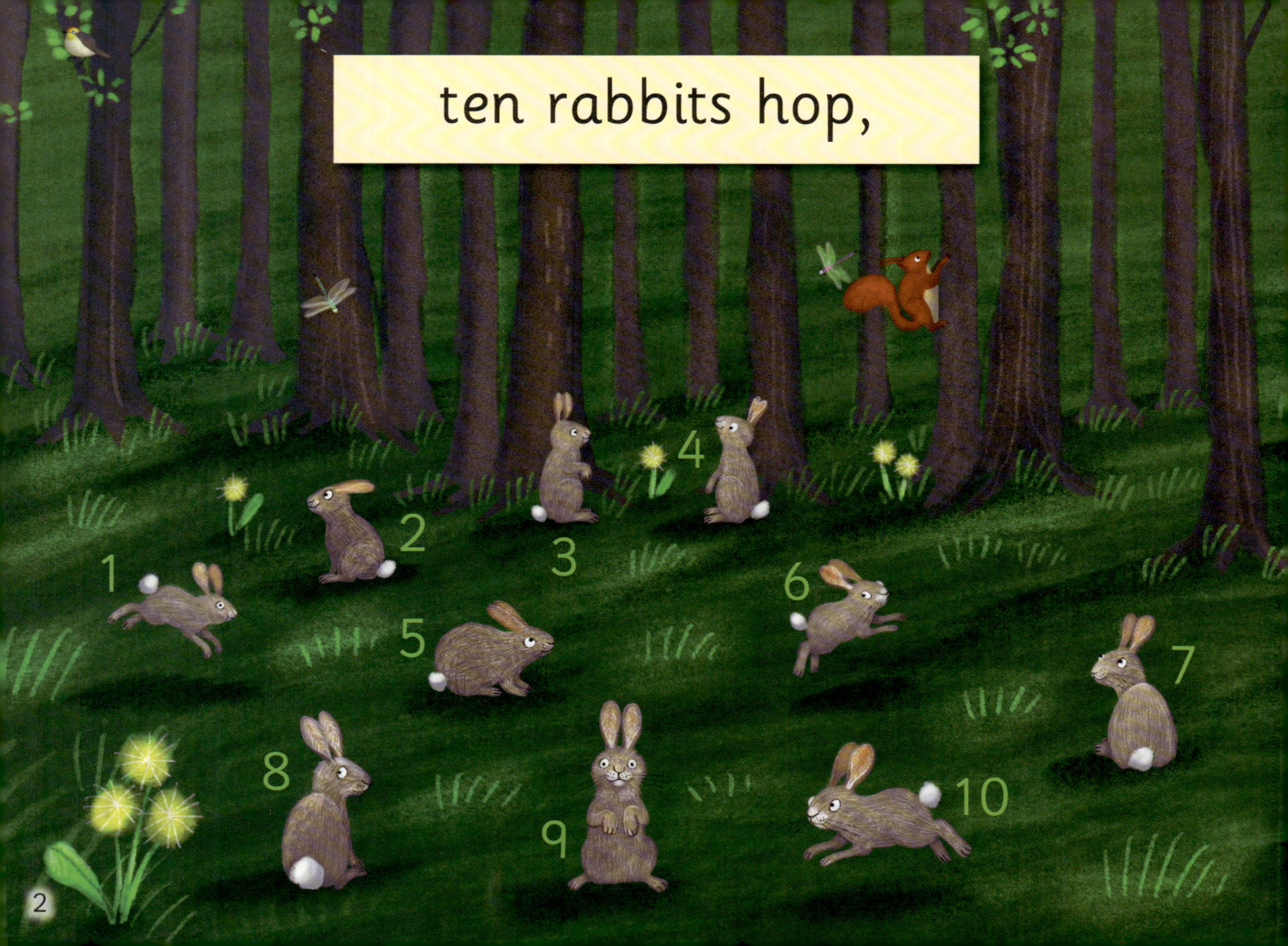

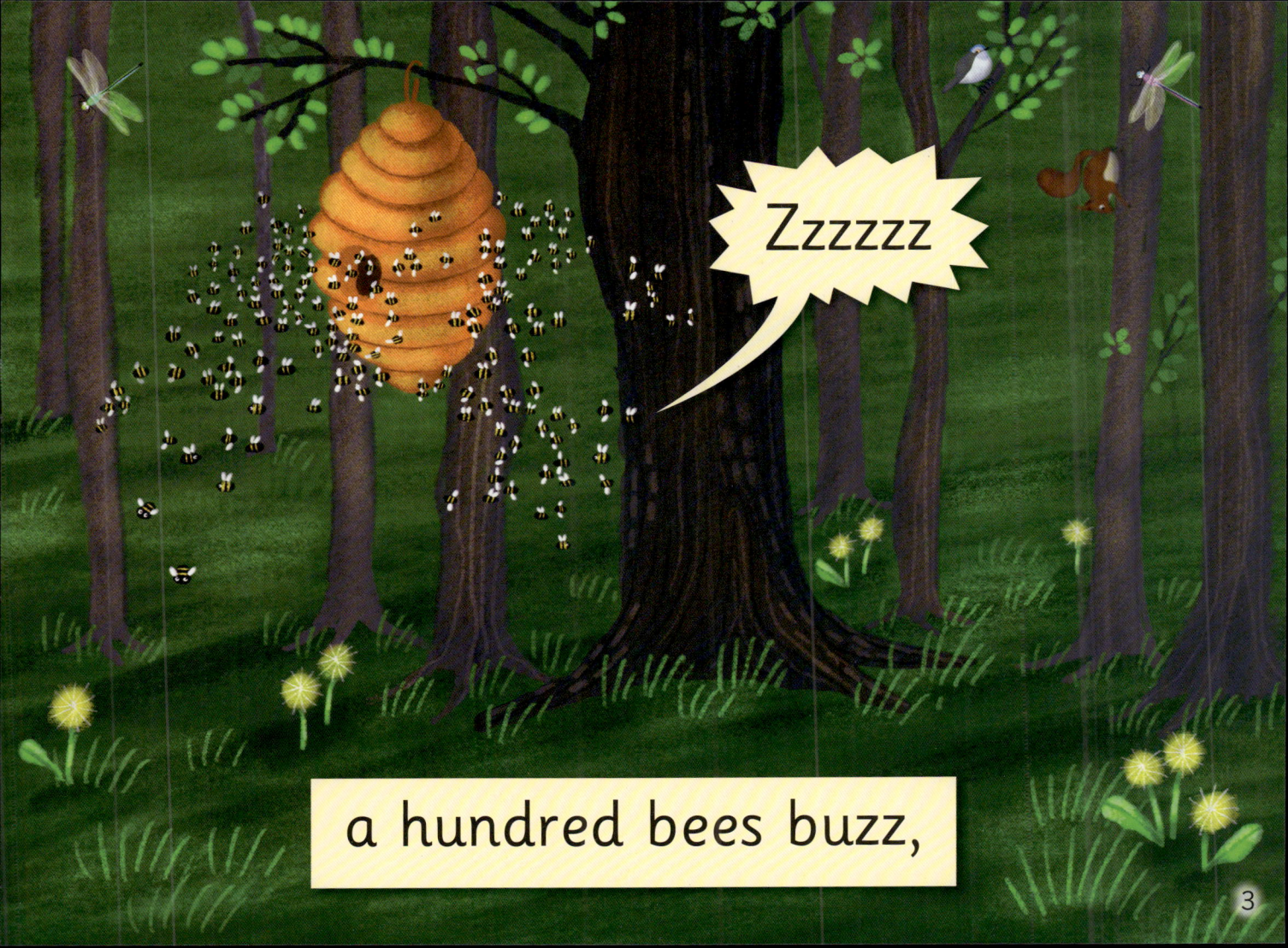

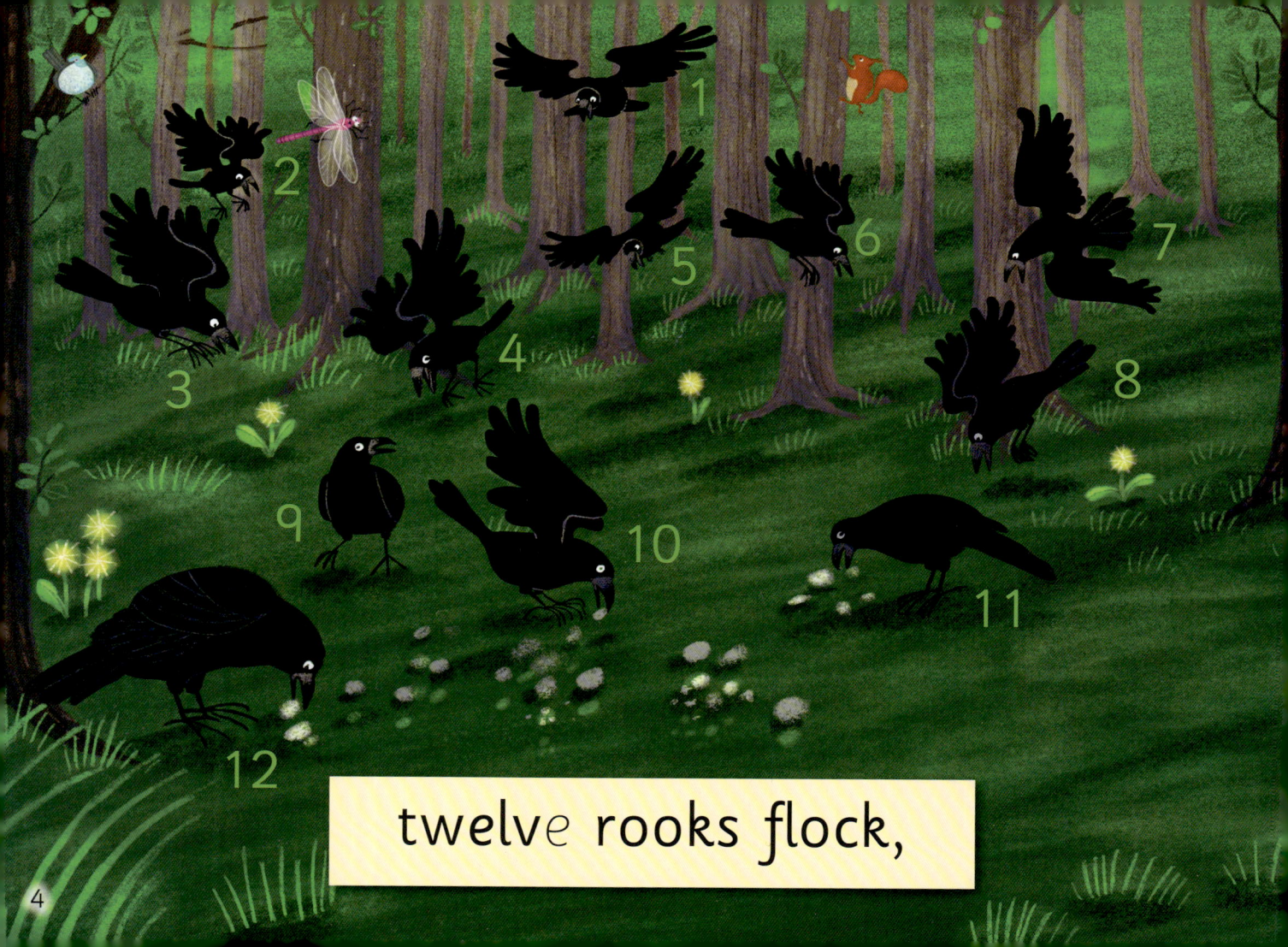
twelve rooks flock,

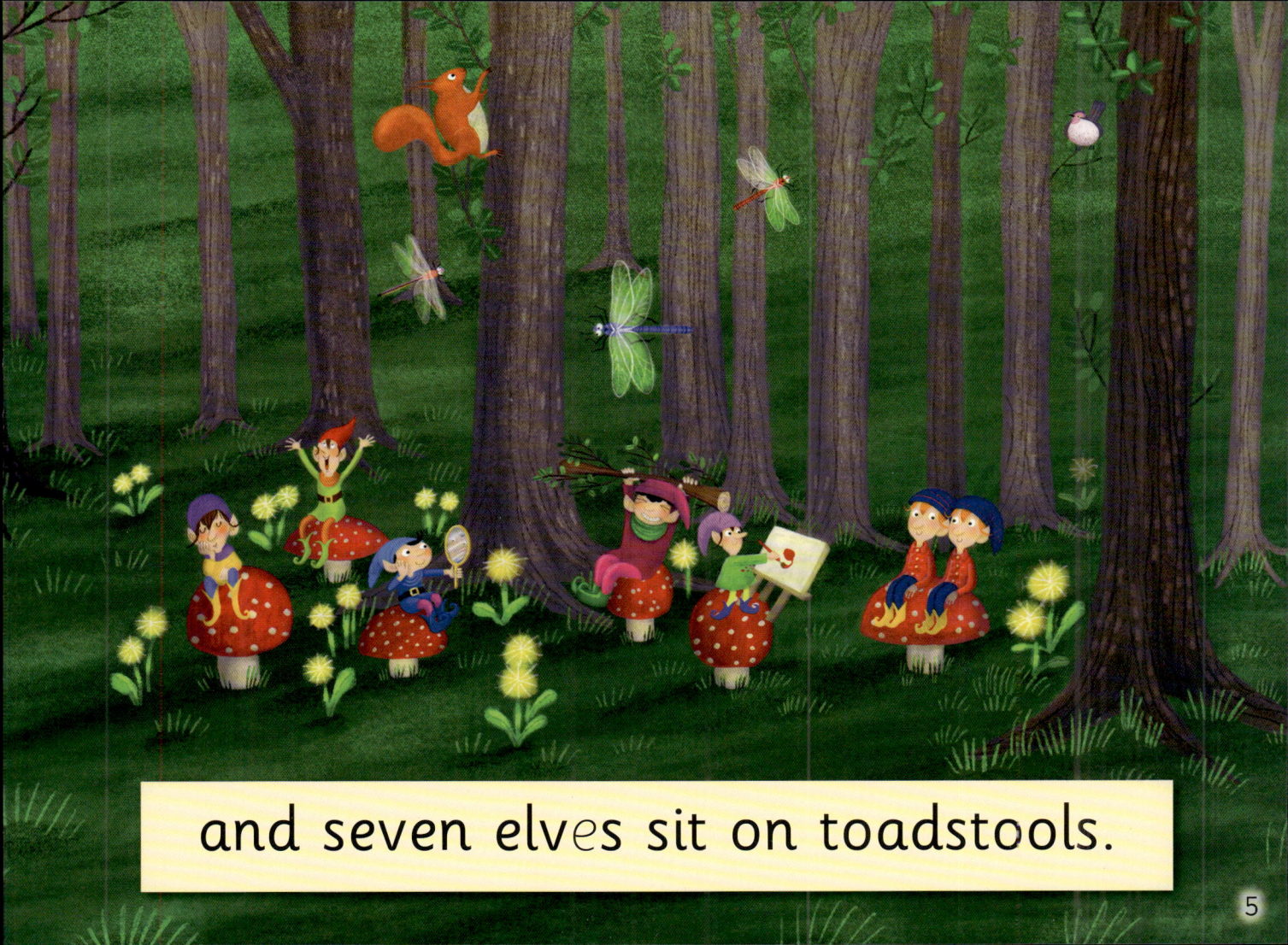

and seven elves sit on toadstools.

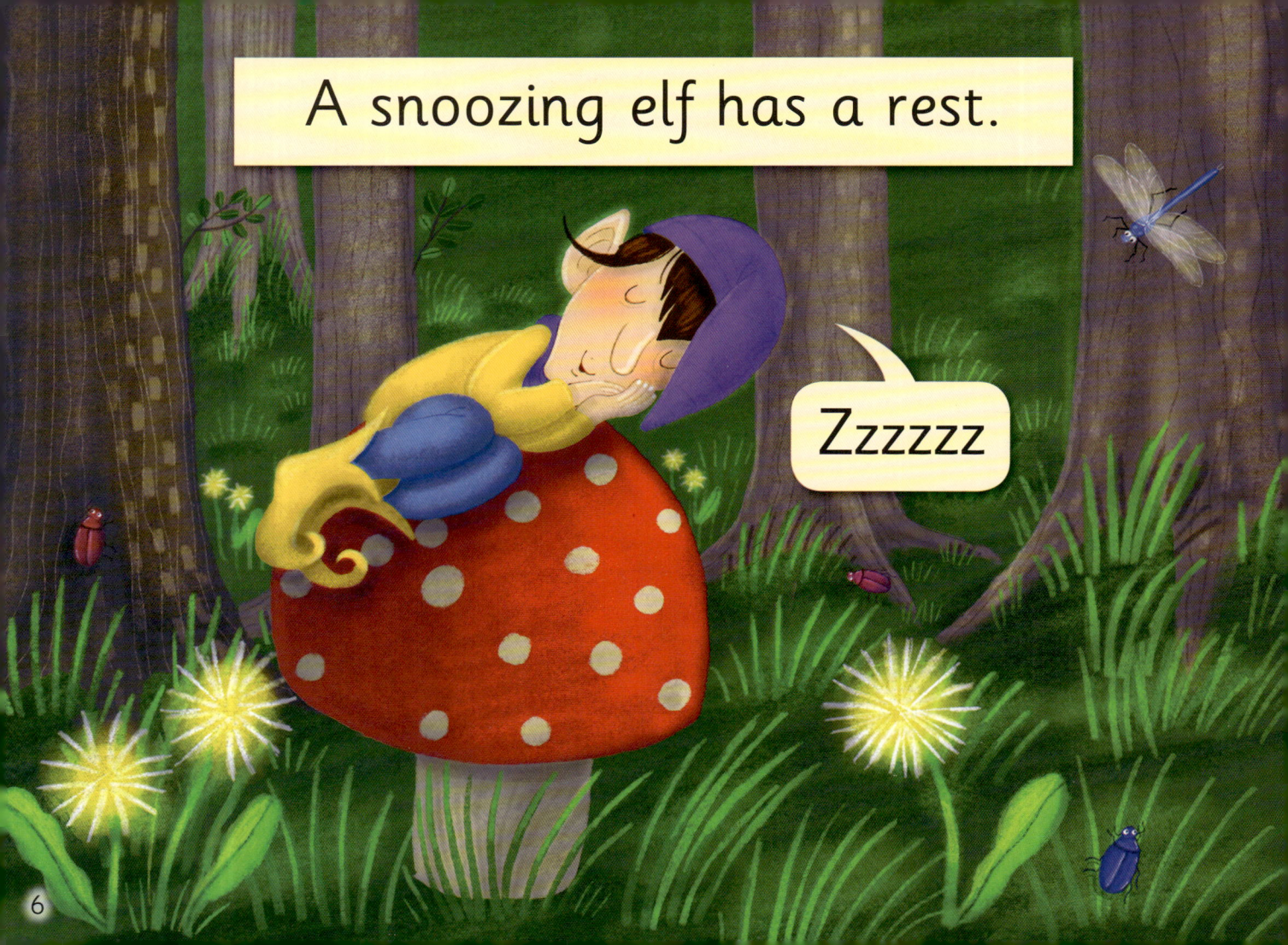

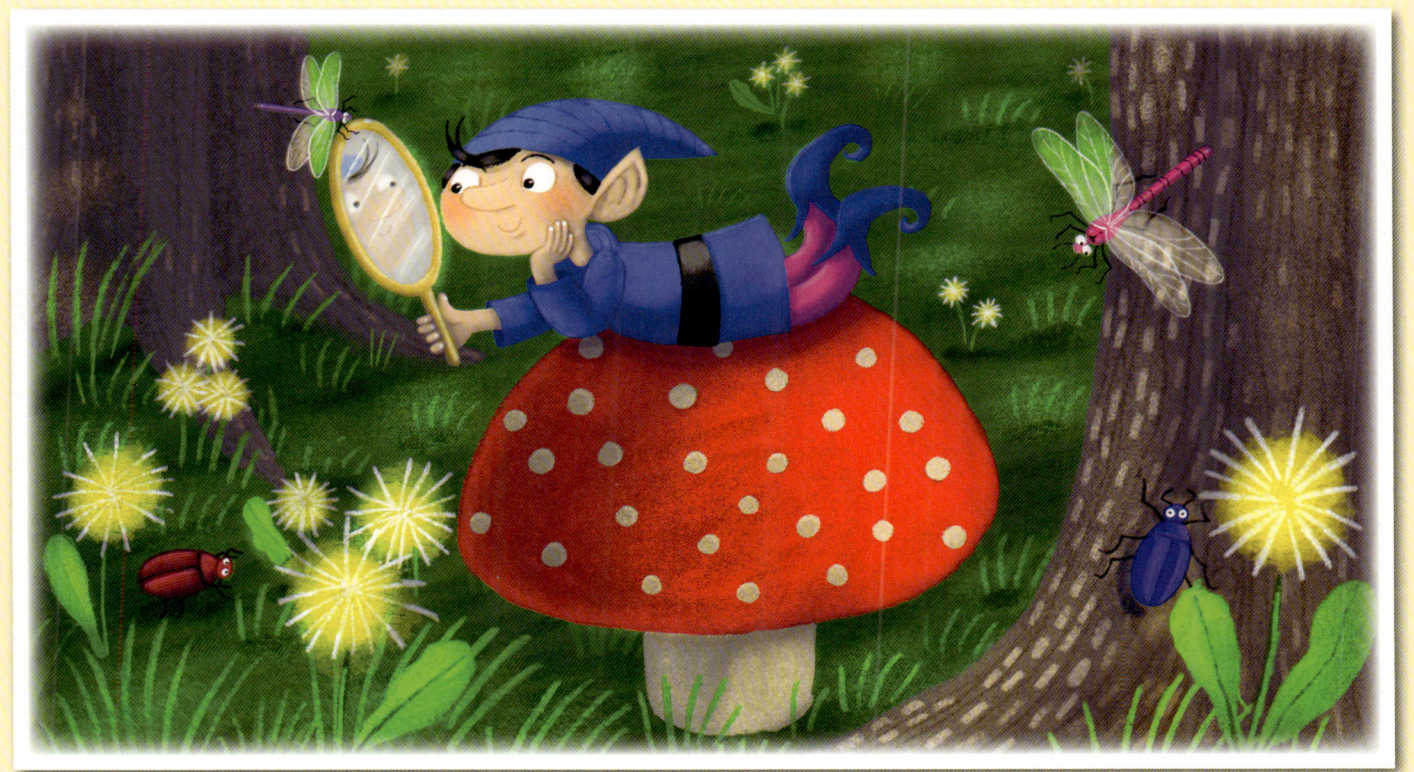

A vain elf looks at himself.

A singing elf hums a jazz song.

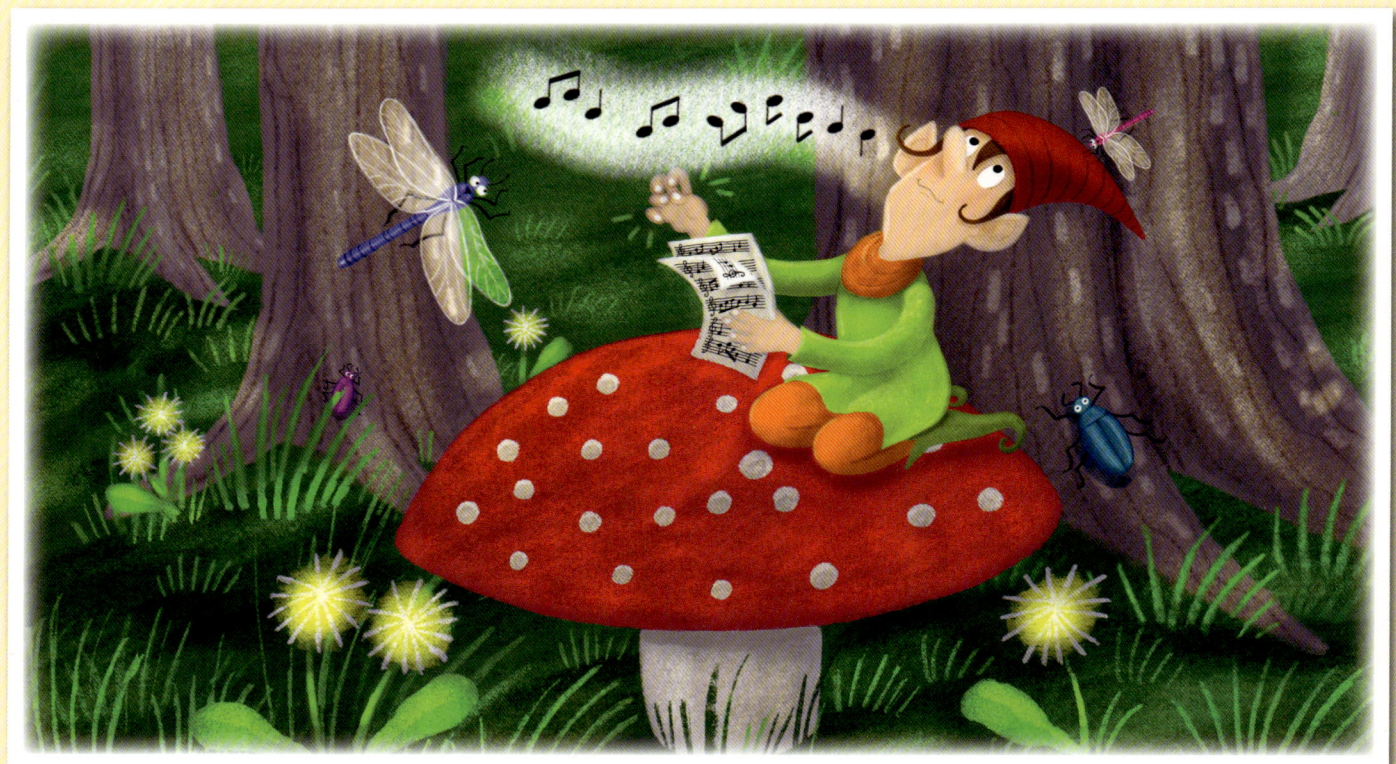

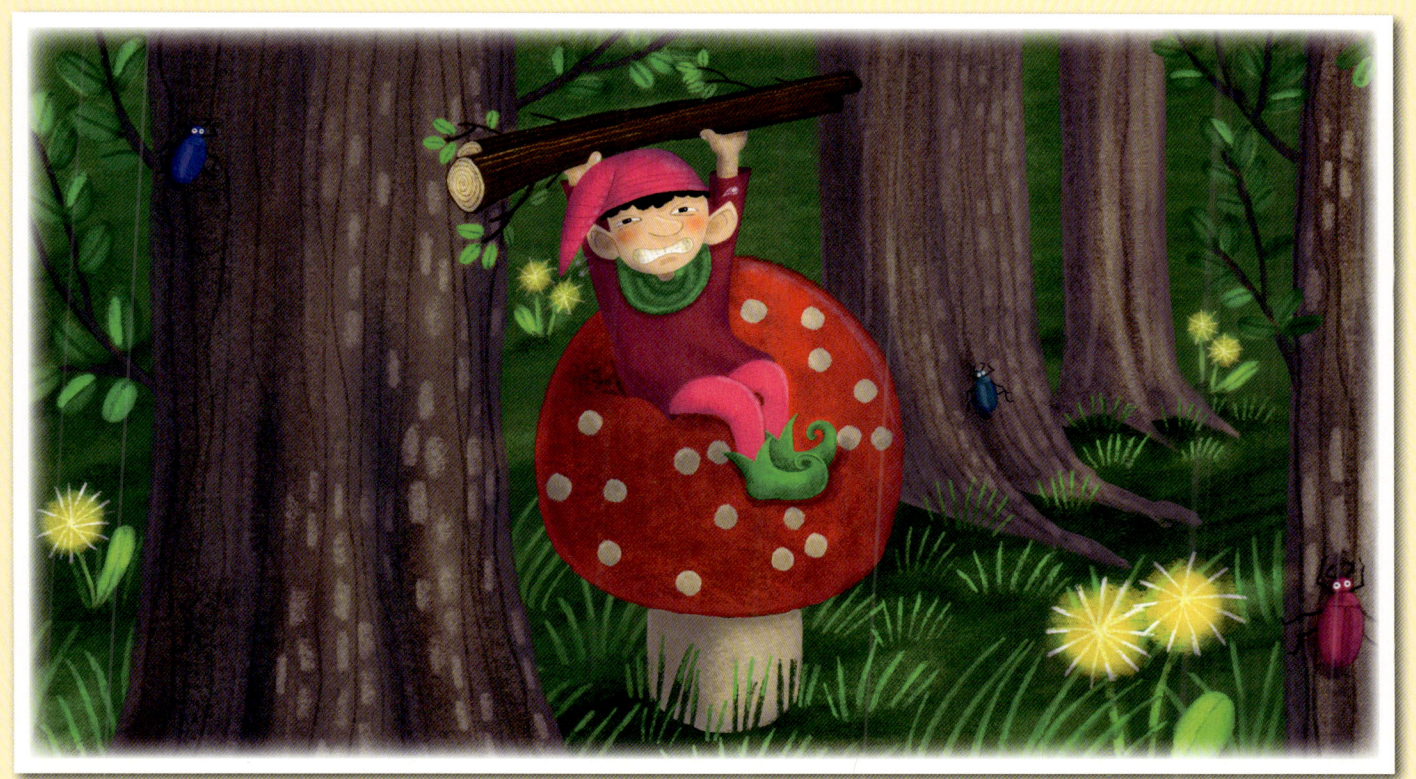

A strong elf lifts up twigs,

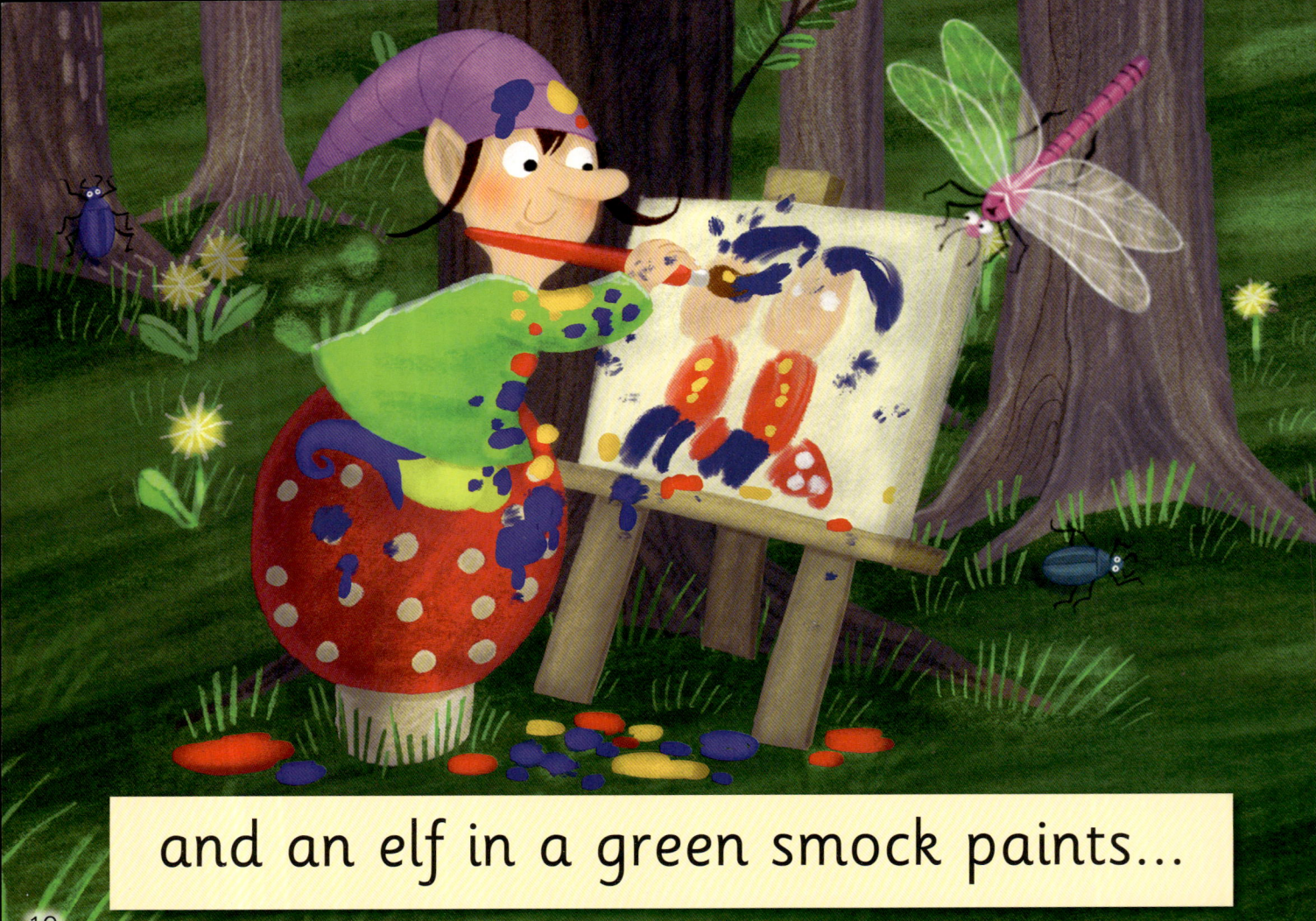

and an elf in a green smock paints...

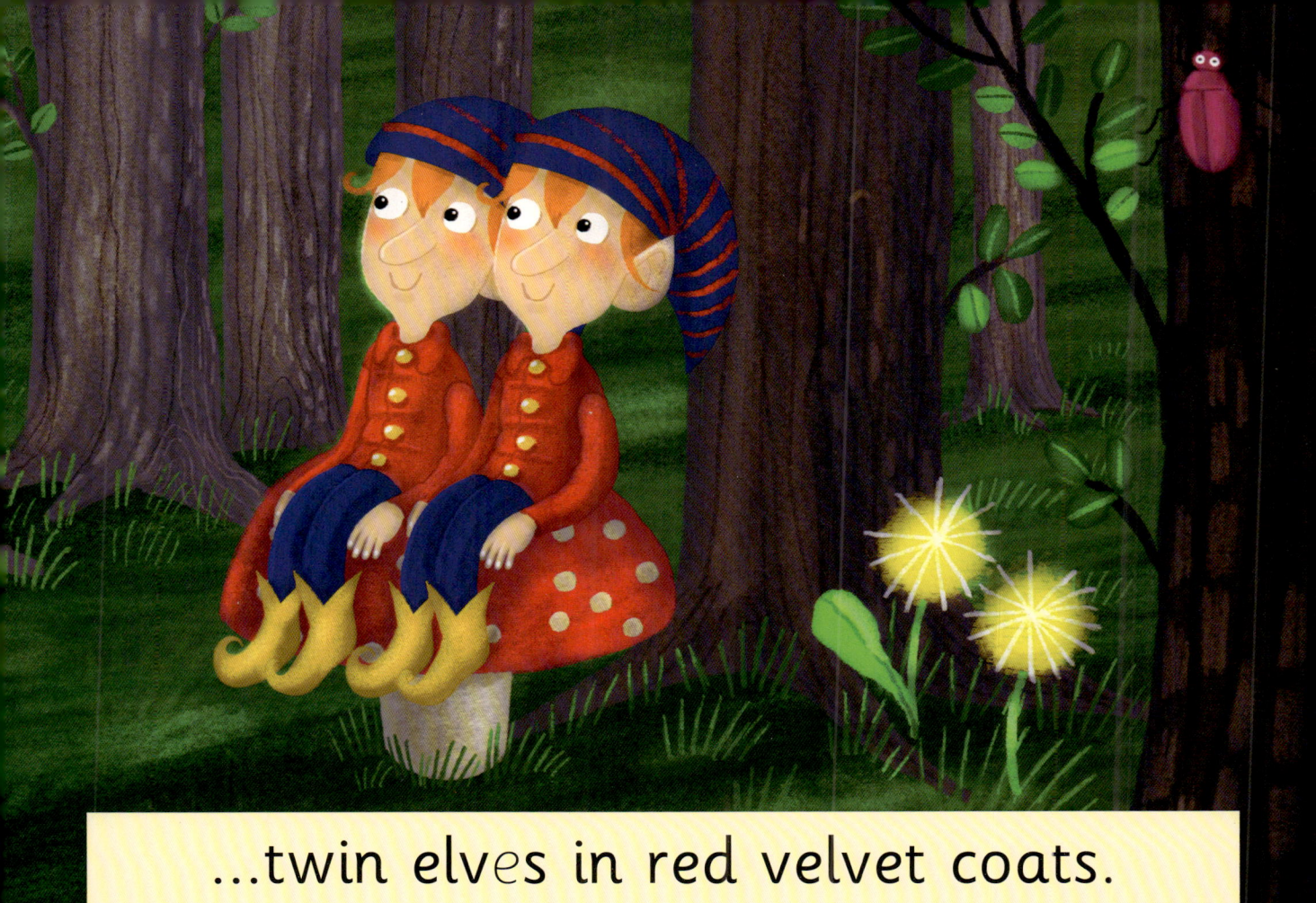
...twin elves in red velvet coats.

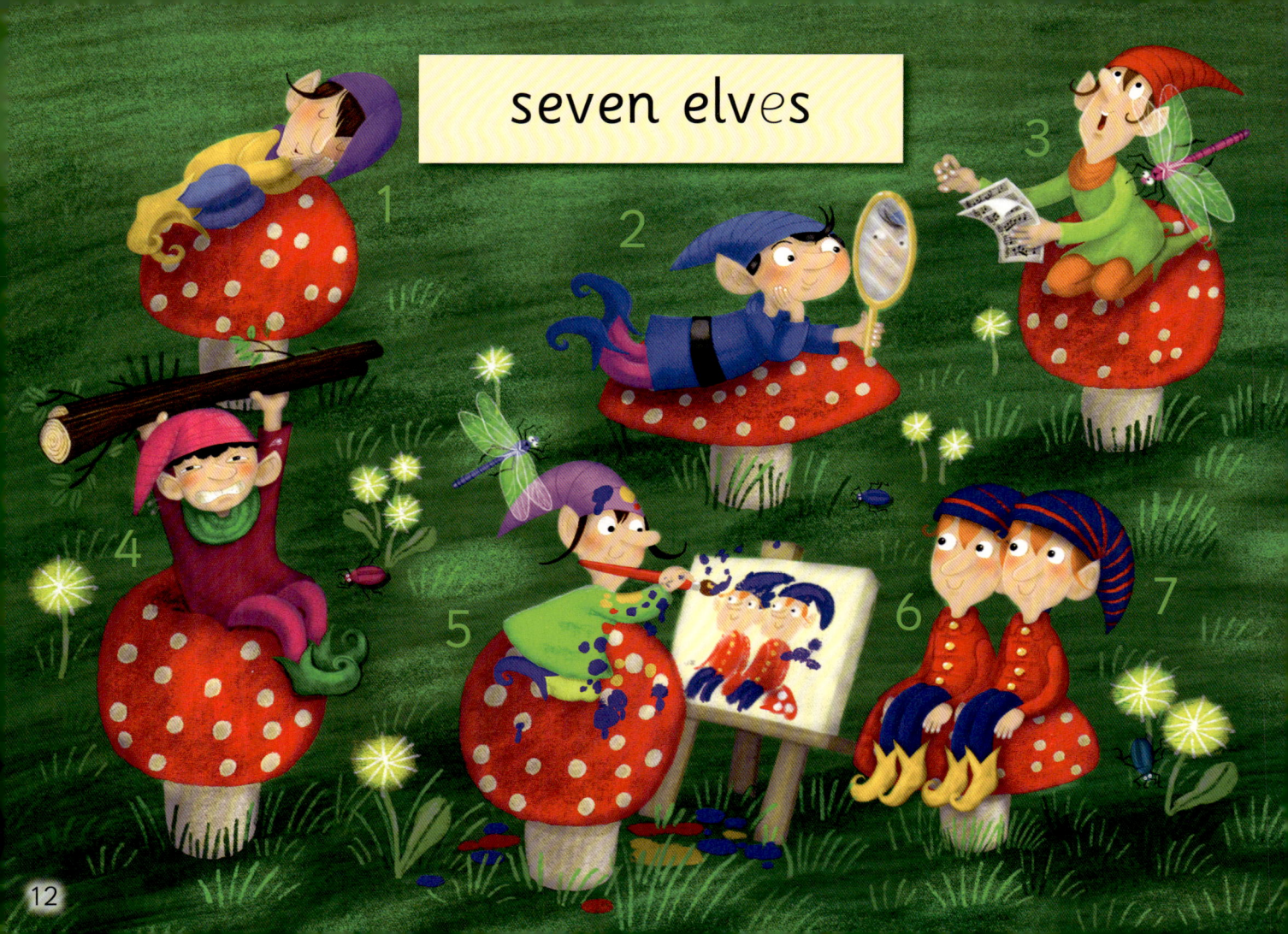